Tips for Reading Together

Children learn best when reading is fun.

- Talk about the title and the pictures on the cover.
- Look through the pictures together and discuss what you think the story might be about.
- Read the story together, pointing to the words and inviting your child to join in.
- Give lots of praise as your child reads with you, and help them when necessary.
- Have fun finding the hidden scorpions.
- Enjoy re-reading the story and encourage your child to say the repeated phrases with you.

Children enjoy reading stories again and again.
This helps to build their confidence.

Have fun!

Find the scorpion hidden in every picture.

Ouch!

Written by Roderick Hunt
Illustrated by Alex Brychta

OXFORD

UNIVERSITY PRESS

Floppy was dreaming that
he was in the desert.

It was hot in the desert.

The sand was hot.
"Ouch!" said Floppy.

Floppy saw a girl on a horse.

The girl was Biff!

"Quick! Come with me,"
said Biff.

"A sandstorm is coming."

The wind blew the sand.

Biff put Floppy on the horse.

The horse went fast.

"Go faster!" said Biff.

"The sandstorm is coming!"

The horse went faster.

"Ouch!" said Floppy.

The horse stopped.
Oh no!

Floppy flew off the horse.

"Ouch!" said Floppy.

"Oh! There's my cactus,"
said Biff.

Why do you think this story is called 'Ouch!'?

Why did Biff make the horse go faster?

Why isn't it a good idea to touch a cactus?

What do you dream about?

Picture puzzle

How many things can you find beginning with the same sound as the 'c' in cat?

Useful common words repeated in this story and other books at Level 2.

coming   fast   girl   said   the   was   went

Names: Biff   Floppy

(Answer to picture puzzle: cactus, cake, candle, car, carrot, cat, caterpillar, cup)

More books for you to enjoy

Level 1: Getting Ready   **Level 2:** Starting to Read   **Level 3:** Becoming a Reader   **Level 4:** Building Confidence   **Level 5:** Reading with Confidence

OXFORD
UNIVERSITY PRESS

Great Clarendon Street,
Oxford OX2 6DP

Text © Roderick Hunt 2006
Illustrations © Alex Brychta 2006

First published 2006

Series Editors: Kate Ruttle,
Annemarie Young

British Library Cataloguing
in Publication Data available

ISBN–13: 978-019-279229-7

10 9 8 7 6 5 4 3

Printed in China by Imago

Have more fun
with Read at Home

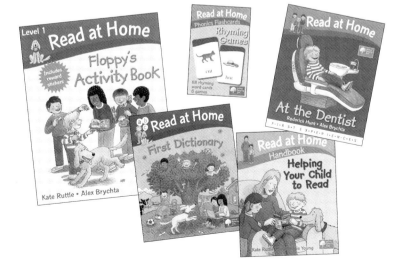